To my parents, Abdulaziz and Dursunay Olgun
—M.O.Y.

To my grandparents
—H.A.

Acknowledgments: My immense and eternal gratitude
to Dr. Ingrid Mattson of Huron University; Imam Khalid
Latif of NYU; The Highlights Foundation; my agent, Jenna Pocius;
my editor, Megan Ilnitzki; and everyone at HarperCollins for their
invaluable input and guidance in the making of this book.
—M.O.Y.

In My Mosque
Text copyright © 2021 by M. O. Yuksel
Illustrations copyright © 2021 by Hatem Aly
All rights reserved. Manufactured in Italy.

ISBN 978-0-06-297870-7

The artist used digital rendering on Adobe Photoshop along with scans of ink
washes, textures, and patterns to create the artwork for this book.
Typography by Rachel Zegar
21 22 23 24 25   RTLO   10 9 8 7 6 5 4 3 2 1
❖
First Edition

In My Mosque

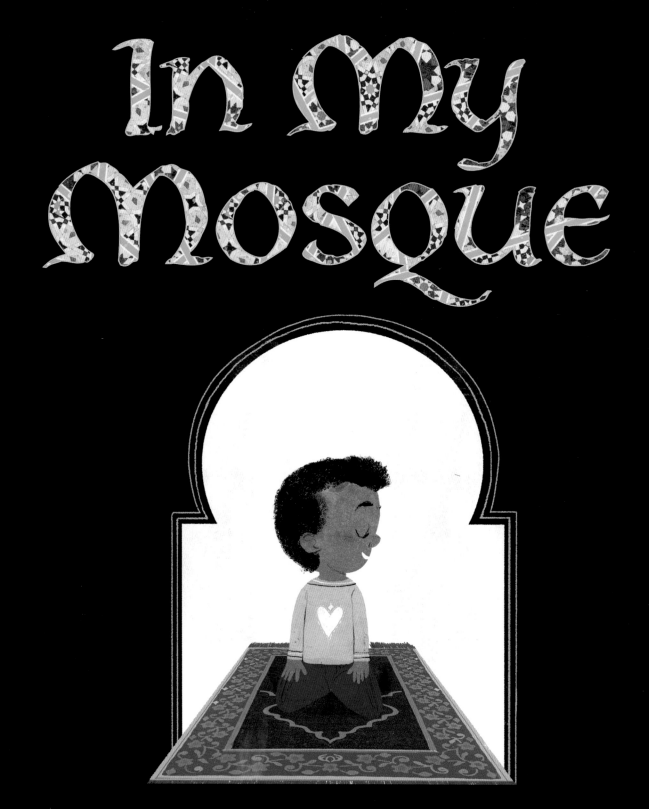

Written by **M. O. Yuksel** ◆ Illustrated by **Hatem Aly**

HARPER
An Imprint of HarperCollinsPublishers

As-salaamu Alaykum

In my mosque, we are a rainbow of colors and speak in different accents. As-salaamu Alaykum—I greet my friends and newcomers too. Everyone is welcome here.

In my mosque, we line our shoes in rows, like colorful beads, before stepping inside.

I wiggle my toes and sink into
the silky-soft carpet.

In my mosque, we dress in our best outfits before standing in front of the most High.

My auntie gives me a hug, and I know I'm loved.

In my mosque, grandfathers nimbly thumb their tasbihs, chanting, **Subhanallah**.

·Subhanallah·

I snuggle up by my dad and listen to the soothing sound of their words mix with the cooing pigeons outside.

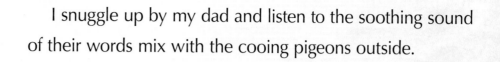

In my mosque, grandmothers read the lines of the Qur'an—BISMILLAHI'R-RAHMANI'R-RAHIM.

Bismillahir-rahmanir-rahim

Butterflies flutter inside me as my friends and I race to see who can spread the most prayer mats and hand out the most tasbihs.

In my mosque, the imam tells us stories of living in harmony, together as one.

I understand—
we are all connected and
come from the
same Creator.

In my mosque, aunties' hijabs sway like a sea of flowers as we move through our prayers.

I try to pay attention, although sometimes I get distracted.

In my mosque, we end our
prayers by greeting the angels on our
shoulders who watch over us day and night.
My angels cheer me on as I whisper heartfelt wishes
and hope they all come true!

In my mosque, we learn to help others whenever we can.

A joy blooms inside me and drifts up like a balloon at the sky-high pile of food donations we have collected.

In my mosque, we eat naan, samsa, and sweet melon slices after prayers.

We zigzag, sneak, peek, and play hide-and-seek in our secret playground. I hope it's never time to leave!

In my mosque, we hug and kiss
each other goodbye.

I look up at the high circular dome
and the pointed archways and my
mosque feels safe like home.

In my mosque, we pray for peace, love, and joy . . .

just like my friends who worship in churches, temples, and synagogues.

You are welcome in my mosque.

ALL ABOUT MOSQUES

A mosque is a place of worship for Muslims, or people who practice the religion of Islam. Islam is practiced by more than 1.8 billion people around the world and is a very diverse, multiethnic religion. There are mosques on every continent except Antarctica and in almost every country in the world.

Mosques serve as a place for prayer, refuge, reflection, and rejuvenation. Mosques may also function as community centers for holiday celebrations, marriage ceremonies, educational and charitable activities, and funeral services. Some mosques, like the Süleymaniye in Istanbul, Turkey, even include schools, libraries, hospitals, bathhouses, soup kitchens, and gardens.

There are many beautiful mosques around the world, with varying architecture and design. Most mosques have tall minarets, or towers, from which the call to prayer is issued five times a day. Inside the mosque, vast open courtyards with fountains serve as places for people to gather. From the airy courtyard, worshippers go inside the prayer hall to listen to a sermon from the imam, the person who leads salah, or prayer. In the prayer hall, there's a mihrab, an ornamental carving on the wall, showing the qibla. The qibla shows the direction to the Kaaba, the first house of worship built by Prophet Abraham. Worshippers face toward the qibla to pray. Decorative calligraphy, geometric shapes, and arabesque artwork enhance the interior of the mosque.

Friday is the holy day of the week for Muslims. Every Friday, people of all ages, genders, ethnicities, and backgrounds attend midday prayer at mosques. The imam reads from the Qur'an, comments on the text, and addresses various topics to deepen one's understanding of the meaning of Islam, such as the importance of good character, ethics, and the value of charity.

Mosques are very hospitable places. If you would like to visit a mosque, simply search the internet for a mosque, masjid, or Islamic center near you and arrange a time to visit.

GLOSSARY

Allah: Arabic word for God.

Allahu Akbar: God is the greatest

Arabesque: Artistic decoration consisting of intertwining, flowing lines.

As-salaamu alaykum: A greeting that means "peace be upon you."

Bismillahi'r-rahmani'r-rahim: In the name of God, the compassionate, the merciful.

Church: A Christian place of worship.

Imam: A person who leads prayers.

Islam: Complete, voluntary submission to God.

Kaaba: The sacred building in Mecca, Saudi Arabia toward which Muslims face during their daily prayers.

Mihrab: An ornamental niche on the wall of a mosque that shows the direction of the qibla.

Mosque: A Muslim place of worship. It is also referred to as a masjid, jamii, or Islamic center.

Muezzin: A person who calls Muslims to prayer.

Muslim: People who practice Islam.

Naan: Round disks of baked bread, also called patir naan in Uzbekistan.

Qibla: The direction of the Kaaba.

Qur'an: The holy book of Islam. It is also spelled as Quran or Koran.

Salah: Prayer performed five times a day during prescribed times. It is also referred to as salat or namaz.

Samsa: A baked Central Asian pastry stuffed with meat or vegetables.

Subhanallah: Glory be to God; God is perfect.

Synagogue: A Jewish place of worship.

Tasbih: Prayer beads.

Temple: A place of worship or spiritual congregation.

AUTHOR'S NOTE

I have been fortunate to attend many mosques around the world, notably in Turkey, Saudi Arabia, Uzbekistan, Azerbaijan, Turkmenistan, Kyrgyzstan, Kazakhstan, Malaysia, Canada, and the United States.

Each mosque I have visited has its own unique architecture and personality. Whether the mosque is large or small, the feeling of serenity and hospitality is the same in each.

I was inspired to write this book after several people expressed their interest in learning about mosques and the types of services and activities that occur inside them. Since Muslims are a minority in some countries, such as the United States, it is not uncommon for people to be curious and even misinformed about mosques and Muslims in general. I hope this book sheds light on this topic and encourages those who would like to learn more about mosques to contact and visit their local institutions. For more information about the mosques featured in this book, please visit my website.

HERE ARE JUST A FEW OF THE MANY FAMOUS AND HISTORIC MOSQUES THROUGHOUT THE WORLD

Asia

Masjid Al-Haram, Mecca, Saudi Arabia

This is the holiest site in Islam, as well as the largest and oldest mosque in the world. It surrounds the Kaaba, the building in Mecca toward which Muslims face during their daily prayers. Up to two million worshippers can be accommodated in this grand mosque during the annual pilgrimage, called hajj, to Mecca.

Masjid al-Nabawi, Medina, Saudi Arabia

Built in approximately 622 CE with the help of Prophet Muhammad, this is the second-holiest site in Islam. Originally made from palm trunks with mud walls, it served as a place of worship, a community center, a court, and a religious school. The mosque has significantly expanded and modernized over the years to include several domes that slide open to shade worshippers. Prophet Muhammad's tomb is located in this mosque.

Al-Aqsa Mosque, Jerusalem

Al-Aqsa Mosque is the third-holiest site in Islam. *Al-Aqsa* means "farthest," referring to the journey Prophet Muhammad made from this mosque on his way to heaven to receive instructions from God.

Bibi-Khanym Mosque, Samarkand, Uzbekistan

A UNESCO World Heritage site, this complex was one of the most magnificent mosques in the world during the fifteenth century. A huge Qur'an stand made from marble sits at the center of the courtyard. It is said that ninety-five elephants transported construction material to build this massive building.

Sheikh Zayed Grand Mosque, Abu Dhabi, United Arab Emirates

This is one of the largest mosques in the world; it can hold over 40,000 people. It is also home to the world's largest hand-knotted carpet. The outside walls get lighter and darker in relation to the phases of the moon.

Great Mosque of Xi'an, Xi'an, China

Built in the eighteenth century, this mosque in China reflects the integration of the local culture and architecture. It does not have minarets but instead resembles a pagoda.

Demak Great Mosque, Demak, Indonesia

One of the oldest mosques in Indonesia, this mosque was built in the fifteenth century and is made from timber. The mosque has four pillars, each carved from a single tree, to support its heavy tiered wooden roof.

Jama Masjid, Delhi, India

One of the largest mosques in India, Jama Masjid was built in the seventeenth century by the Mughal emperor Shah Jahan, who also built the famous Taj Mahal. Mughal-style mosques have elaborate circular minarets, pointed arches, and onion-shaped domes.

Shah Faisal Mosque, Islamabad, Pakistan

This mosque is shaped like a tent, surrounded by four tall minarets. Considered the largest mosque in Pakistan, it is located in the picturesque foothills of the Himalayan mountains.

Africa

The Great Mosque of Djenné, Mali

Built in the thirteenth century, the Great Mosque of Djenné is one of the most famous landmarks in Africa and a UNESCO World Heritage site. An annual festival, which includes music and food, is held to repair the mosque from damage caused by rain and humidity. Kids help by stirring plaster, then race to see who will be the first to deliver the plaster to the mosque.

Kutubiyya Mosque, Marrakesh, Morocco

A landmark structure of Marrakesh, and a classic example of Moroccan architecture, this mosque is surrounded by gardens and has a minaret so tall, it can be seen from eighteen miles away. The beautiful prayer hall has a hundred pillars that support horseshoe-shaped arches. Built in 1147, Kutubiyya is also called the Booksellers Mosque because it was once surrounded by book shops.

Al-Hakim Mosque, Cairo, Egypt

One of the most famous historical mosques in Egypt, Al-Hakim has the largest open courtyard in the country. It is coated in white marble, rectangular-shaped, and framed by beautiful parallel columns. Al-Hakim is also home to the most ancient and unique minarets in Egypt, attracting tourists far and wide.

Europe

The Blue Mosque, Istanbul, Turkey

Its official name is the Sultan Ahmed Mosque, but it is more popularly known as the Blue Mosque because of the more than 20,000 handmade ceramic blue tiles that decorate the inside walls. Its six minarets set it apart from other mosques, which usually have four. During summer nights, a light-and-sound show is held in the park surrounding the mosque.

The Grand Mosque of Paris, Paris, France

Built in 1926, the Grand Mosque of Paris is the largest and oldest mosque in France. It has a school, a library, a conference room, a garden, a restaurant, a tearoom, a hammam (Turkish bath), gift shops, and prayer rooms that can fit 1,000 people. During World War II, the mosque played a vital role in helping British soldiers and Jewish families escape from the Nazis.

Mosque of Rome, Rome, Italy

Built in 1995, this mosque contains classrooms, a library, a conference center, and an exhibition hall. The interior is embellished with beautiful palm-shaped columns that represent the connection between Allah and the individual worshipper. Repeating geometric designs and glazed tiles with the Qur'anic phrase "God is light" decorate the walls.

Great Mosque of Córdoba, Córdoba, Spain

Orange trees bloom inside the courtyard of this grand mosque, which was built in the late eighth century. The interior of the mosque is full of striking horseshoe-shaped columns.

East London Mosque, London, England

This mosque holds annual 5K runs for fitness and fun, and to raise money for charity. It also participates in environmental issues like climate-change marches. The mosque contains a fitness center, a radio station, a nursery, a library, multipurpose rooms, offices, and classrooms.

North America

The Diyanet Center of America, Lanham, Maryland, United States

Located on Good Luck Road, this mosque has an indoor pool, fitness center, gift shop, exhibition hall, restaurant, and even a Turkish hamam. The complex hosts conferences, festivals, picnics, educational programs, and holiday celebrations.

Al-Rashid Mosque, Edmonton, Alberta, Canada

Built in 1938 with funding from diverse ethnic groups and religions, this mosque actively promotes interfaith understanding by providing educational events and guided tours for the public. The mosque offers many academic, recreational, and social services to the community, including a day care center, a preschool, leadership seminars, and senior citizen clubs.

South America

King Fahd Islamic Cultural Center, Buenos Aires, Argentina

The largest mosque in South America, it includes a gallery for exhibitions, a campus with two schools, a restaurant, an underground parking lot, and sports fields. It also has its own weekly public radio program.

Oceania/Australia

Lakemba Mosque, Sydney, Australia

This mosque is one of Australia's largest. During holiday prayers, this mosque attracts over 30,000 people. It welcomes non-Muslim members with exhibits and barbecue parties during Australia's National Mosque Open Day.

SOURCES

◆ Bodden, Valerie. *Mosques*. Mankato, MN: Creative Education, 2008.

◆ Frishman, Martin, and Hasan-Uddin Khan, eds. *The Mosque: History, Architectural Development and Regional Diversity*. London: Thames & Hudson, 2002.

◆ Khan, Aisha Karen. *What You Will See Inside a Mosque*. Nashville, TN: Skylight Paths Publishing, 2003.

◆ Maqsood, Ruqaiyyah Waris. *Islamic Mosques*. Mankato, MN: Heinemann-Raintree, 2006.

◆ Nason, Ruth. *Visiting a Mosque*. Twickenham, UK: Cherrytree Books, 2005.